MADHUSUDAN BHASKARAN

MY CHILDHOOD'S TAPESTRY

ISBN
Paperback: 979-8-89929-252-1
Hardcase: 979-8-89961-594-8

This book is a work of fiction, hence any resemblance to actual people, living or dead, events, incidents, and places is purely coincidental.

Acknowledgements!

Thank you **Sangmitra**, for lighting up the fire in my belly through constant, consistent, even persistently nagging follow-ups.

This book is a consequence of your successful persuasion to use my creative writing abilities to better personal effect—far away from the professional world, where they had made a considerable dent. **This book is for you!**

Special thanks to you, **Kavita**, for editing and proof-reading this manuscript, and transforming it into publishing-ready material.

Couldn't have taken this big leap of faith without either of you.

Contents

First duel

My parents tell me it was a hot and sultry day at my mother's place in Kerala.

And there I was! Thrust into this world to go through its varied trials and tribulations. So, I bore it the way we humans always do—by crying, rebelling, and then by embracing it happily, tackling a myriad of fears in the process.

Time flew; not that I remember any of my baby years, except for some indelible imprints in my memory drive that could never be reset, despite innumerable reboots.

One such vivid incident was a fight sequence with another classmate when in kindergarten. While the reason for the quarrel is still foggy, it blew into a fistful one even before the seeds of reasoning could germinate on the fertile soil of innocence.

In the blink of an eye, we were rollicking in the mud, pulling hair, raising hands, biting, and trying just about everything to get rid of the other from the face of the earth.

Before victory could be sealed from either side, the principal, made aware of the commotion outside, separated us and put us through a masterclass of physical, hand-to-hand combat that I am sure neither of us could have ever been capable of meting out to each other. Our duel ended unceremoniously; sheer fear of the autocracy forced us to shake hands.

Frenemy

A couple of years later, I found myself in a quaint convent school that symbolised all the uninhibited trappings of modesty, respect, and trust.

There were close to eight classes in a day, including games. This may sound funny to some of the readers, but yes, our classes started with a moral science session where the 'sisters' and teachers talked about sacrifice, love, and brotherhood through their life experiences.

A plethora of virtues, such as kindness, cleanliness, honesty, and respecting elders were imbibed in us through quotes and adages imprinted strategically on the school's walls and notice boards—the most famous and common one being—honesty is the best policy!

I alternated between science, social studies, games, and physical education all through my pubescent years, hating with all my heart, the former two and loving the latter two, in equal proportions.

As you can make out by now, divine intellect never shone its light on me. Apt to say then that I never passed any class with flying colours. In fact, I managed to just scrape through them, missing the dreaded red colour by a wafer-thin margin. I still suffer from nightmares where I see myself falling through the precipice of failed grades and ending up in a downshifted class. All my friends happily sail through, leaving me haplessly flaying my arms to catch that proverbial straw that could lead me to them.

Adding fuel to this nightmare fire were my real-life classmates. Life was slowly teaching me its wicked interpretation of 'wolves in sheep's clothing'. I had so inherently gotten fed up with the zeroes, and the soreness all over my body due to the consistent physical battering at home that I started doing what every smart lad does—hiding my examination answer sheets from the prying eyes of my parents and forging their signatures on the papers.

Confidence at that age is innate and fear is absent. Going to play with fellow friends after hiding the test papers was a constant in my life. Conscience did not suffer from any of the inhibitions that stop you dead in your tracks on the highway tread marks of ethics and morality. Soul-cleansing thoughts were never invited nor were there any doors left open for them to be welcomed. In fact, they were trampled into the concrete pathways before they could even rear their moral compasses.

Remember the adage, "No bad deed goes unpunished" from the moral science classes? In comes the friend in a wolf's garb, who, after seeing me busy playing my cover drives in the stadium, treacherously reaches my home to his 'uncle and aunty'. He has sighted a killing, and he is going to make the most of it.

Between dollops of snacks and drinks being propitiously and abundantly offered, he casts his devilish shadow with an utterance that sounds like, "We got our test paper today, Aunty, (with greater emphasis here) and I got 8 out of 10."

Observing the sudden gaping chink in the armour, the enemy moves in for the final kill. The merciless sentence does it all: "Aunty, I think your son got a zero." And then the absolute annihilation—"Aunty, didn't he tell you?"

The hand and the spatula that were about to serve the third helping froze midway, the eyebrows arched upwards, the smile angled down, and the small, yet visible, twitch of the lip signalled the arrival of the impending catastrophe.

His job done, the dear friend departs to his abode, on a bloated stomach, leaving my mother to wait for her son to come back from his sojourn.

Having no idea of the fists and fury that awaited me at home, I happily tread back, satisfied and proud of the half century that I hit, to make a winning case for my team. Mom greets me with the same candour, albeit with her hands behind her back. Rest is history.

The permanent marks on my body bear testimony to the treason and still remind me of the vagaries of misplaced trust in friendships.

Sportingly yours

I was fortunate to have been blessed with an alternative medium that showcased my mettle, which otherwise would be lost in the empty annals of study books and childhood nightmares.

The moment I entered the sports arena, a perpetual halo, albeit invisible, seemed to follow me everywhere. Athletics, cricket, hockey, football, and basketball were my constant companions, post school time, till late into the night.

Unlike nowadays, our residential layout offered a plethora of sports grounds, all to be used for free, by anyone interested. The challenge though, was to reach the venue early and guard it from all those who made a run for the courts and pitches that these beautiful stadia had to offer.

Who better to hold that fort than 'yours truly'—the one person who was famous for treating studies and all matters of the school's papyrus with utmost disdain.

My teammates had more pressing challenges to address, such as preparing for the next day's exam. I pitied them since I gleefully distanced myself from such lowly sufferings that humanity had somehow embroiled itself in.

I had also attained Nirvana by then, thanks to mom's incessant beatings—they had opened my dormant 'chakras' and along with them, the truth that pain is fleeting, though mighty hurtful.

So, I self-nominated to be the keeper of the venue—not to the chagrin of my fellow mates but instead, to their great joy.

If the match was to start at four in the evening, I would be there by two in the afternoon. Sun, rain, fog, nothing could dissuade the professional in me. Pacing up and down or doing my jogs, I would guard the venue like the zealous lion that protects its pride under all circumstances.

When the match started, my latent talent invariably shone through. Maybe, because all others had used up their mental faculties studying for the exam and were now incapable of doing anything worthwhile. But who cares? This world was my stage, and I had a pivotal role to play.

My love for the rotund instrument that was used to hit goals, three-pointer shots, fours, or sixes seemed mutual. I could hit it at will, with a single foot, wrist, or swing action when I demanded. The physical form of the leather or rubber was inconsequential.

Looking back, sports was that one friend who understood my fear of education as an occupational hazard. It, hence, willingly conjoined with this existential pain, forming an unbreakable, intangible companionship, transcending the mere physical to the non-frivolous metaphysical.

It kept the scoreboard ticking and with it, somewhere, somehow, my own motive in life.

Outstanding

There she was! A miracle of nature when she first came upon my sight. A single ponytail, beautiful teeth with their unevenness taking my breath away, ironed school dress (a rarity for lesser mortals like me), and the infectious laughter that passed the corridors of school and reverberated through the gardens of my hopeless heart. A lover alas was born!

She was a topper, and I couldn't even find my standing in the bottomless pit. A diligent analysis done with utmost perfection by my very happy frenemies, against my absolute volition, showed me squirming through the depth, albeit surely landing uncomfortably a few feet above the abyss of zeroes.

But who was to stop my one-way love? My heart pounded when she was called for a beautiful rendition of a choir song, when she topped the class, and when she celebrated her birthday in her yellow dress.

That's how love is, isn't it? It has to go through its own devilish sieves, filtering through the quiver to pull out that one arrow which when shot bears the hallmark of marksmanship that Cupid is so famous for.

My heart's cacophony peaked when she never bothered to look at the unkempt guy staring blissfully at her. Unfortunately for me, at that very moment, the bespectacled Geography teacher ,who was teaching us about the Sahara Desert, saw me. And the temperatures peaked on both sides!

With a strict nod of her head and a peripheral glance that would have put an eagle to shame, she goaded me to stand out in the corridor where every trespasser, after having a serendipitous glance at me, could disavow my presence.

Upon my questioning her, "Why should I stand out?", she gently replied, "because you are outstanding". The raucous laughter that bellowed around me broke my heart with no saviour in sight. What shattered me though was the conviction that my love's laughter was mingled with that mass dissemination of joyous rapture. She, sadly, was one amongst the many happy folks there who just wanted to see me 'stand out'.

She couldn't be blamed though; phantoms are just those—fleeting apparitions.

My love for her thus invariably died an early, painful death buried under the scorching, unrelenting sands of teenage shame.

Cupid had missed his mark, by a stupendously long, immensely wide margin. The aftermath was equally devastating. Anything on Sahara, even its mere mention, still gives me sleepless and sweaty nights.

Branded siblings

I was the youngest in my family. My parents' life seemed to have upscaled a few years post my birth, with some creature comforts sneaking into our small two-bedroom house.

Unlike today's world, where most of the kids are treated like kings, we, many a time, were toasted on the frying pan, or in the fire of household wars, and sacrificed on the altar of accusations.

Punishment was relayed through a variety of home-grown instruments that left blue blotches on our frail bodies. We were then temporarily laid to rest in a locked bedroom, to be released only when tempers receded.

I was the more mischievous child—loud and uncouth—the outgoing one, overtly fighting the fight for friends and family alike, taking the cudgels on their behalf to ensure unbiased justice. The smallest of wins had to be aggressively and haughtily showcased.

The failures, on the other hand, were to be silently strangled and buried in an unmarked grave. Unfortunately, when you are known for your vociferous brand style, the unusual silence becomes deafening to all, sowing seeds of doubt. When caught, the punishments thus seemed fair.

My brother was my opposite, the silent predator scoring his wins at will, without sharing the limelight. No one knew he even existed; seen one second, gone the next. When he failed, he was nowhere near the scene of the crime. No fingerprints to match, no culprit to be found, or punished for the wild misdemeanours.

Who was then the probable culprit? Me, of course; the more vocal, more overt, more on-the-face guy. The gavel would invariably fall without a chance of a plea bargain ever.

As the punishing cane rained its ungodly pain on me, my brother would watch silently, wanting to stand up for the truth but fearful that his brand style would take a beating. He would then let go with a visible grimace, eyes promising to reward me for this sacrifice with some goodies.

We spent a lot of our childhood days playing these proverbial cat and mouse games, the 'Jerry' in him invariably besting the 'Tom' in me. Regardless, both of us shared a great bond based on mutual understanding, respect, and camaraderie. In this rollercoaster ride, the seven-year age difference never mattered.

He was my lifeline, my first port of call. And I was his friend and friendly foe; both rolled in one.

A pocketful

Our family of four was always a close knit one; Papa was the bread winner and Mumma, the home giver. While he diligently worked to give us money for a good life, she indulged us with her selfless care and companionship.

Roles were well-defined, even in the absence of markers, to show where one's role ended, and the other's started. It was a fluid, but well-entrenched framework based on family values, compassion, and the need to provide the best for each other.

Behind this vestige of normalcy though, there was trouble brewing in paradise.

Adolescence comes with great personal expenses—expenses to trumpet your wealth, expenses to tackle peer pressure, expenses to treat friends, and most importantly, expenses incurred to impress. We kids were growing up!

Add to this bucket of woes, the concept of pocket money was non-existent then. It was not even a privilege or entitlement; at best, it was a mere failed hypothesis. Pockets were meant to carry only peanuts, jaggery, sweets, bus tickets and others, as required; some of the trousers did not even have them.

That did not deter us; we had to at least try to ask for our right to pocket money. Parents were providers, after all. My brother decided to go first, given his seniority. His well-rehearsed narrative nailed it, leaving me fuming and berating as always.

It was easy for him to unflatteringly demand his ask, given his seemingly calm countenance, respectful disposition, and gainful spending habits. It was no surprise then that my parents readily agreed.

Mine was a different story altogether. My rugged face, curly hair, steel spectacles, coupled with my non-existent soft skills ensured devastation even before I uttered my ask. One look from my parents snapped my mouth shut and left me cowering internally. I realised then that just as in life, there was no second chance for the same opportunity.

I went back to the drawing board—unwilling to give up—materialising a plan. My book now tore at irreparable places, my shoes scuffed, my trousers ripped, my spectacles broke. Money started getting distributed between both my parents to take care of this sudden spurt in realistic expenses. And with it, my piggy bank bloated and belched when needed— the money that I siphoned off post repairs ensured that.

This success was short-lived though; the unnecessary overheads and incidental expenses ensured that.

Kaleidoscope

Our residential colony was a paradise tucked within a leafy suburb in the capital city of one of the largest states in the Republic of India. Being a railway society, residents came from across India, and this kaleidoscope of myriad cultural convergence made this county a little heaven.

Religion, caste, creed, colour, and all such Civics callouts were non-existent. Agarwal, Mathew, Patel, Gupta, Mirza, Mehta, Saxena, Mehrotra, Paul, Das, Mukherjee, Ali, Chatterjee, Rao, Nair, Baig, Pillai, Mudaliar and many more such surnames lived and worked amicably in this small world—happy with their nine-to-five jobs and families.

As is the case with most organisations, official hierarchy was necessarily prevalent, but it automatically vanished post crossing the gates of the society, on the way back home. Selfless friendships effortlessly blossomed thereafter.

It was not uncommon for favours to be given and taken as part of the office setup. Not surprising, given the world that we lived in then was fundamentally a very helpful and transparent one. Opportunism, selfishness, and pride were relegated to a small, irrelevant corner. It would take them four decades or so to rear their vicious heads.

The official demarcation was gauged from the houses that people lived in. The higher the position, the bigger the house, the more elite the neighbourhood. You could make out the status of the residents from the dresses they wore and their communication style.

Childhood is a great leveller; most of the children from across this railway society studied in the two schools established within the gated community. This included the thoroughbreds as well. They played, studied, fought, hugged, and cried with us. Our lives gradually entwined and with that, their homes.

For us children, food was the sole way of scraping the vastness of the Indian cultural cauldron. Nair would bring idly, Rao bisibelebath, Mehrotra aloo parathas and pickle, Ali biryani, Mukherjee luchi aloo, Paul egg sandwich, Saxena gobi aloo, and so on.

I would reach home smelling of an eclectic mix of the food partaken, with no aromatic remnants of the dosa or the sambhar that I had carried. Instead, the lunchbox would be cluttered with the remains of this finger-licking multifaceted Indian cuisine.

It was at that very moment that the true beauty of the Indian diaspora shone through magnificently.

The trio

We were the 'famous trio' like the three-girls' 'Triad troop' that used to walk the streets of the colony during our school years. Sometimes, our paths crossed.

The three of us, though diametrically different in most aspects, always stuck together, because of a common congenital problem—one martinet parent.

While most classmates were unanimous in their outlook of our loathing for books, we looked inwards towards home to get the transitory encouragement that all was fine. The futility of this dream though, was amplified by the reality of the ruthless marking that our test papers endured.

The problem was further magnified by the fact that irrespective of the changing marking systems, new teachers, or home tutors, our marks remained obstinately unaffected. They never even plateaued on the graphical wagon of results—in fact, they went into a perilous descent. This translated into nightmarish consequences for us in our now not-so-peaceful abode.

We, therefore, started looking outside for comfort and reassurance. Eventually, in this world of misconstrued brilliance, we found each other—three misfit souls, fit for each other.

We belonged to different states—one from the hills, the other from the north of India, and I was from the south. We lived a mere ten-minute walk from each other; this helped us immensely because our brilliantly-strategised plans needed our physical proximity for their successful execution.

As per our planned design, when we were to watch a movie in the theatre, we would convey to our parents our intent to visit a dear friend whose mom had suddenly taken ill—a social initiative by the look of it. That friend for obvious reasons lived far away—and at least one bicycle was needed for the triple ride.

The money for the movie was cunningly arranged from the piggy bank that mom had, from under the mattress where papa kept loose change, from inside the rice containers where some notes were tucked away for emergency purposes, and very daringly, even from the back pocket of papa's trousers that hung in the cupboard. This modus operandi was a regular feature, shamelessly owned by any of us, whenever the apt opportunity presented itself at our respective homes.

We would then regroup at a common rendezvous point with the bicycle in tow. The absence of all kinds of communication gadgets was an added blessing; no fact-finding missions were ever possible by our elders.

Triple riding was the unsaid norm, since it gave all of us equal opportunities for hard work and a fair share of the dividends of our labour. Diversity and inclusion are a big thing now—we misfits lived them, then.

A special exception though was made. The friend who brought the bicycle was given a shorter distance to ply—ethics and equality, now a standard practice in corporates, were the cornerstone of our relationship. Again, we misfits were intelligent enough to accommodate this very early into our working relationships.

Movie done and dusted, we rode back in silence, reminiscing the efforts, the journey, and the five-hour escape from the tight-fisted home reality that now waited with closed arms.

Nonetheless, for the 'famous trio' brotherhood was for keeps—one for all and all for one!

Frenemy tamed

The 'famous trio' could never be caught; or so we thought.

On one of the many successful sojourns to the city to watch a movie, under the stereotyped pretext of a friend's mom being unwell, we ran into a turbulent, uncontrollable storm when we reached our respective homes. This was a departure from our normal routine of success and flummoxed all three of us.

The uncountable whacks, curses, and threats of being thrown out of the house continued for a week. We finally got the opportunity to meet far away at our usual secret hideout to discuss the ramifications of this loss. Most importantly, we wanted to figure out how the impossible leak had occurred.

Post brainstorming for two days and reliving that fateful day and a couple of days before that, we suddenly found the beginnings of a chink in our armour.

Remember the frenemy who used to come to my home to discuss my math marks? Yes, the same guy who used to help himself to my food and then stab me in the back; it appeared that he was at it again. This time he had played the three of us, increasing his circle of subterfuge.

One of us slightly remembered seeing him or his doppelganger on the way to the movie theater. Given the unsurety of the recognition, he thought it prudent not to share it with the rest of us. There was no need to sound the alarm, therefore. That was a mistake, given that the frenemy had sounded the war bugle.

We were shattered to the core, and our dream of independence had died a fast, yet excruciating death. Overtaken by anger at this unforgivable deceit, we cycled furiously to his house, intent on confronting him for his sins and punishing him for his turpitudes. As was the practice those days amongst us teenagers, we fruitlessly called his name from outside the gate. The foe did not bother to come out and face us.

Not intent on giving up, we rang the bell, smug in the knowledge that he was sulking inside, afraid to face not one, but three of his nemeses. After all, we had reached him without any advance warning—exactly the way that he had so ruthlessly trampled on our short-lived joys.

His mother opened the door, and our rehearsed excuse left her unsuspecting. She innocently called out to our 'traitor' to meet his dearest class buddies. After all, we had come to return the money that he had so selflessly loaned to us in time of our need.

The turncoat approached cautiously and maybe sheepishly as well. The moment he crossed the doorstep, we hugged him tight, keeping him between us, and marched him down the stairs. A furtive glance behind us showed his mom in near tears at this endearing show of lifelong friendship.

Downstairs, out of the visible range of his mother and the house, and a few blows later, the truth cascaded like a waterfall; it was exactly what we had envisioned. He had made the trek to each of our houses, told our moms that we were at least ten kilometres away from the targeted house of our hypothetical friend and

God knew why we were where he had sighted us, especially when there was an exam the next day.

We learnt quickly that luck could change at twisted angles, angles that can literally break your back—just like life, in all fairness.

Five-year plan

The average middle-class life during those times was both challenging and interesting. Neither our pockets nor our money ran deep. Thankfully, most of us belonged to the same strata of society and the artificial trappings of money never enslaved us. Instead, we were stitched together by the same sense of uncluttered solidarity that exists in the armed forces.

Unlike now, we children never got what we asked for, at least till the third time around. The ask was always dug deep into the soils of budgetary constraints that seemed to last a lifetime but ranged between a few years to never.

If fortunate, a new set of clothes adorned our wiry bodies once or twice a year, depending on the festivals that we celebrated; in our home, it was mostly during Onam. This also depended highly on the remaining monthly budget, post the money order to relatives back in Kerala. After all, their monthly cash burn ritual hinged on this perennial postal delivery.

The shirt that was passed down to me was never my choice, thus—it was at least two sizes larger than mine and instead of clinging to me, it draped on me. On a breezy day, the wind would somehow find its way inside it and transform me into one of those heavyweight wrestlers that we see on television. If anybody dare punch me, all they got was a fistful of air that escaped with a whoosh sound.

The bell-bottomed trousers did not fare any better. They were two waist sizes more than mine and unsurprisingly, while walking, would gather the dust from the roads and gracefully carry it. My feet could never be seen; they could only be felt in them.

The belt would travel twice around my waist before it could find its final resting place. Counting the holes on the belt was unnecessary since the belt was littered with the ones made by the cobbler to adjust to my slim waist. The original belt was unrecognisable the moment it changed hands.

My foot size was never even a matter of conjecture. The discounted shoe, with the bigger size, came home to adorn my feet. The fist-size gap at the ankle was fastidiously filled with cotton or a discarded cloth, with a prohibitory warning not to run too fast.

When the soles ran afoul, the nearest bicycle repair shop had enough rubber to renew their vigour for another couple of years. Consequently, without too much effort from my side, the next five years saw my height increasing by a foot or so in my 'layered' shoes.

In retrospect, life was weirdly funny for us children. Nehru's five-year plan for India was still around. Our parents had earnestly imbibed that concept, refurbished it, and executed it on us with great precision, adding salt to the wounds of our already heavyset childhood.

In my case, focus was on sizes that could last for five years.

Milky way

I had a morning chore that needed to be completed untarnished; to get fresh milk at home. For that to translate into good health for all, I was given the onus of visiting the cattle shed early in the mornings. The brief was simple—bring the milk refill in our regular can back home, without spilling a drop.

This whole endeavour looked good on paper and even mildly exciting; the responsible boy would wake up at five in the morning every day, take a bath, eat breakfast, don his school uniform, take the bicycle out, and ride into the early sunrise to the milk vendor's thatched cottage, about three kilometres away, one way.

At closer scrutiny, this daily routine was fraught with a lot of challenges from start to finish. First up, I had to wake up early in the morning. I was a sportsperson who played till eight in the night, perfecting his shots. Coming back home, I had to tackle my everyday adversary—the school assignment. Being right brained, I could not decipher what the intent and the outcome of the assignment was. I would, therefore, spend close to a couple of hours to come up with a unique answer that none in the class had.

Second, for the milk man, the whole process of milking the cow, collecting the milk, and distributing it amongst the crowd of customers that gathered took about two hours from start to finish. If I was lucky, I would be the first few to get the milk. If not, which was most of the time, I had to bide my turn, which came post all the aged morning walkers—who had nothing better to do than wake up and walk—were done with. I would eventually be left with a half an hour window to reach school, post home delivery of the milk container.

Third, while it was easy to cycle with an empty can, returning home was nothing short of dangerous. I had to balance the heavy milk container on one hand, off the handlebar, ride on the potholed roads that were, by then, brimming with school vans transporting children to our school. It was a grand prix ride, with all the necessary twists and turns, hairpin bends, and the obtuse angle that I had to sit for compensatory balance.

One bumpy ride, and the milk, having a mind of its own, dancing and undulating, gurgled out of the container, leaving a trail on the road that could lead anyone back to my home. By the time I reached my abode, the initial two-litre can would have lost its weight by a somewhat big margin.

The more heart-wrenching issue was that my one-sided love's house was on the way, just after a left turn that took me to the milk vendor's home. When I started my journey, the early rays of the sun prevented her from waking up. There was no way I could steal a glance then.

The only hope was while coming back home since it was close to school time and being the girl that she was, punctuality was her special forte. If I was lucky, I would see her on the balcony drying her wet hair while studying from a book that I did not believe was from our grade.

The moment I would see her my machoism took over inadvertently. I would let go of my feet from the foot pedals of the cycle, take that dangerous, steep turn without my hand on the brake, holding the worrying, dangling container that promised to throw all of its insides out on the road.

The problem was that whenever I did these mindboggling acrobatics successfully, she was nowhere to be seen. The rest of the audience would run helter-skelter berating me for this lame act.

When it finally happened, and my love crossed the road, the bicycle unexpectedly behaved suspiciously, as if it was fed up with my domineering nature, the handlebar wobbled, the pedals furiously spun on their own, and I lost my balance.

The cycle twisted at an odd angle and instead of staying on the road, diverted into a bushy, prickly hedge that was the cornerstone of all the houses in the colony. The cycle let go off me, the momentum throwing me straight into the hedge with my head leading the way, and the milk container broke free, spilling everything on the road.

Fortunately, my honour was intact, without rapidly fading into sheepish oblivion. My love passed me by without even a glance. While my entire body was outside, my head remained stuck inside—recognition hence was impossible. Taking me to be one among the many vagrants who bothered her with their silly antics, she walked away.

Luck had played a punishing joke on me when I needed it the most. Destiny's cruel hand was dealt literally by dad when he saw me in my drenched uniform, broken cycle, empty container, and bruised face. The rest as they say is history, well remembered by me.

Failed promises

Post office hours, dad had this ritual of sitting on a reclining chair on the verandah of our attractive house, reading the newspaper and assimilating global events for that day. He was an avid reader who started from the masthead and ended up on the last news of the sports page that used to signal the end of that newspaper edition.

This, though, did not mean that he was not privy to the happenings around our colony and inside his house. Over a cup of piping tea, post return from office duties, his first port of call was mom, who waited impatiently to share the daily impish deeds of the younger son. Each day she had a different story to tell in a new packaging, with similar, if not the same, mundane physical consequences.

Perpetually, it was about my grades, either for the unit tests, or the main exams. While these marks had the uncanny knack of hovering around the early or the mid-forties, the only solace was when they were compared with the results that my best friends obtained; by providence and sheer willpower, they too never fared well. God bless the 'famous trio'!

The main bone of contention for my parents was the absolute annihilation of our reassuring promise that we would end up with a ninety percentile. We could even end up as toppers, if the teacher was unbiased in her marking. This guarantee was given consistently by us. It's a different story that never once in our school lifetime were we able to honour that word.

There was another niggling problem. We always sounded the war bugle against one of our neighbours, a strapping miss who spoke less and promised nothing. Any question on her preparation would end up in a squeamish, teary-eyed monologue that fundamentally hinted at her perceived lack of preparation or grey cells.

How then could this lass, who shivered literally in her boots every time she gave exams, be a competition to us? She was a nobody, an easy guinea pig to be showcased as an opponent worthy of our proclaimed promise. Not that she had anything to do with this exercise. She was blissfully unaware of the benchmarking in the households of her secret foes; she remained friends with us, hence.

The exam results were a different story altogether. Shockingly, she would have wrested the ninety percentiles from under our very proud noses, leaving us with fragments of marks, leftover after all had taken their due share. The acidic rub would be when she approached us during our collective mourning time and placated us with sweet words of consolation.

Our parents were fed up. They knew innately that these rogues were just hyperventilating but the belief in marvels forced them to walk through this thorny, swampy trust path recurrently.

Parenthood itself is a miracle; its resilient belief never once gave up on us.

Seven-year itch

Both of us brothers were never good at studies. It could be our lack of interest, or the lack of concentration, given our tender age.

Our method of studying was also contrasting in style. My brother was definitely the more intellectual of the two. His concentration abilities were phenomenal and well known in familial circles. He just needed ten minutes to demolish a chapter or a book and remember near verbatim what it was all about. Incidentally, spending too much time on schoolbooks was not a comfort that he relished very much. Those ten minutes were a rare occurrence, sighted very close to the exam dates.

My brain's competency was nowhere even close to my brother's. I had to spend a minimum of a couple of hours to understand a concept, let alone grasp the intricacies of what the chapter had to offer. I would be fretting and perspiring before, during, and after the exams, given this serious lack of intellect.

All this wouldn't have been of significance had it not been for the career-making examinations that we had to appear for, post our schooling. India was still considered a third-world country, missing the fancy frills of the so-called first-world countries found towards its west. This necessitated the need to latch on to whatever known career avenues that the country had to offer, however minimal they might be.

There were primarily two career paths of any value for us students to settle down in life—Engineering and Medical. A huge percentage of us had to vie with each other to get into the prestigious institutions offering these courses. Not getting into them meant sounding the death knell from a psychological standpoint—the penetrating gaze of the colony folk branded the non-entrants as failures immediately.

We knew that these intense career-defining examinations were not for us. Given the external pressure, we had no choice but to follow the majority of our peer group, even when we were morally against it. Thankfully, we had not subscribed to Biology, so Engineering was the leftover choice.

A month or more would be spent filling in the relevant admission forms for the various engineering institutions, paying for them, and post confirmation, trying to study for them. The charges for the forms and the preparatory tutorials were paid by dad. Being the sole investor, he had vague hopes of us getting through some of the lower-ranked engineering colleges, even if it was to help mom save face within the small, but very observant, female community.

We had other plans. We had done everything that our parents asked us to do. So, our moral compass did not suffer from any major guilt pangs. On the exam day, we would, in all earnestness, leave home at the said hour, and supposedly reach our exam venues, or so it seemed.

The cat jumped out of the bag sooner than expected. Of all the days, one of our dad's colleagues chose the very day of our entrance exam to buy sweets from a famous sweetmeat shop near the city's railway station; nothing wrong with that.

While paying the bill, he chanced upon my elder brother happily engrossed in munching the many delicacies that the shop had to offer. The nice elder approached my brother cautiously, still unsure of his sighting, given that the latter was supposed to be at some place more productive. The reaction of my brother, from what I heard, was worth a million untold words. Caught red-handed and with no place to hide, the prodigal son returned home on a full stomach, riding pillion on dad's colleague's bicycle.

I never believed in the theory of probability till very much later and under the same circumstances, the same scene unfolded with the same gentleman, the same restaurant, the same exam, and with the same result.

The pillion ride was faster this time around, given that dad's colleague's bicycle was replaced by the then ubiquitous Bajaj scooter. The dreaded drive home for me was over in the blink of an eye.

This was seven years apart in manifestation—with a more terrifying outcome, given the repeat.

Little Gavaskar

The playground in front of my home was not a very big one. Nonetheless, it served my purpose of playing cricket and badminton.

Cricket was my first love, though. When the cricket bat owner was absent or just vainly proud, given his control over the game, badminton became my forced second choice. There was a cemented court for it with a worn-out net that could hardly save the shuttle cocks from flipping to the other side, given the velocity and force of our wooden badminton racquets.

For cricket, the reins of the day's play were owned by a single person—the one who owned the bat. Cricket balls could be borrowed from friends and foes alike. They could be bought as well since they were relatively cheaper and more in abundance. The manufacturing component did not matter—leather, cork, rubber, plastic—all were game for us.

Cricket bats were a different ball game altogether. Between the ten of us friends there was only one person rich enough to have a bat and wickets to call his own. He, thus, called the shots when it came to play time, toss, run out, no-ball, wide, and everything else in between. We would turn into mute supportive spectators when he ruled the roost for obvious reasons.

Every afternoon, I would practice with a plastic ball at home to hone my bowling skills and use my mother's washing block of wood as my bat to prepare for my batting, the prowess of which had to be showcased in the evening.

Climbing up the guava tree in my compound, I would sneak a peek towards the ground to check whether the bat owner had made his appearance at the agreed upon time that day. If he had, I would feverishly climb down like a monkey, wear my slippers, and rush to the playground.

If he was absent, there was nothing else to do but to wait for God to listen to my prayers and beseech him to come. This rarely happened, given his mother invariably won the argument with the lord and dissuaded him from sending her son to play. That day would be the worst day of my life. It meant going back to the study table at home, while listening to the sounds of the other group laying claim to the ground and playing their game of cricket.

Sadly, the bat around which this whole waiting game revolved was not a new, strong, complete block of wood with the typical company logo on it. On the contrary, it was just the opposite.

This bat was decades old, maybe even grandfatherly in countenance, broken at the handle, with wood giving way to cracks that would painfully engulf your fingers within them when you hit a shot.

Additionally, a portion of its bottom had, I am sure, eroded leaving only three-fourths of it available for use when playing. It was more of a triangle than the normal rectangle that we were so accustomed to seeing. Slip positions were mandatory because the chances of the ball kissing that perforated side were greater than finding the middle of this well-weathered bat.

But tough times called for tough choices. This bat was my most beloved. Playing the waiting game was never a complaint. Caressing it made up for all the other pains that I endured. With the bat in hand, I was in poetic motion, playing my shots with wanton glee, and more often than not, finding the fence.

When I looked around, I would eye an aged Sikh gentleman who was our neighbour, watching me concentratedly from outside the ground. He would applaud my drives and praise my defensive techniques. He would stay glued till I was at the crease. This singular fan base gave my batting more reason to excel, and my chest swelled with pride.

He used to call me 'Little Gavaskar'. While I was not even remotely close to that legend, this moniker was my confidence booster all my life when dealing with bouncers, yorkers, and any other unplayable deliveries.

CEO in the making

Mathematics was my Waterloo, literally. I always had the urge to drink water and go to the loo every time the school bell sounded to remind me of this class. I would invariably be the first in the class to raise my hand and ask for permission to visit the restroom.

Congruency, permutations, binomial, algebra all seemed to have descended from the Greek gods' constituencies and their funny sounding names were nowhere amusing in action. In fact, they were the most treacherous, traitorous weapons of 'math' destruction ever to be unleashed on unsuspecting souls like me. My parents were blown away by the avalanche of zeroes that I received in my class tests hence.

While I was busy fighting the battle of my life with this fire-emanating enemy dragon of a subject, there was one guy who was sailing through all this—blissfully unaware of the turbulence around him.

For him Math was hope, relief, love, friend, and guide. Moreover, it was the 'knight in shining armour', protecting him from any bad grades that Hindi and Sanskrit threw at him almost always. He was a colossal mess when he appeared for those other subjects. Math was his saviour; he could fight the world with this weapon by his side, wielding it with practice, a trained eye, and demolishing any opponent brave enough to oppose him. The glint in his eye outshone everyone else's when it came to Math—his favourite subject.

Beaten humans like me could only be awestruck by his intellectual magnificence and implore that he be our neighbour during the morbidly calamitous exam day. My prayers remained unanswered; I would end up sitting towards the end of the classroom, with just the blank wall for company.

The Math teacher was not that adept, but to my limited brains, she was the only one who could give serious competition to this boy. Given her position in the class hierarchy, she had the undue advantage of calling the shots. She could decimate any of us with her larger-than-life red ink if we dare cross her teaching or pose questions on her solution to assignments that she wrote on the blackboard.

I hardly even bothered going on that path because one vicious stroke from her pen would ensure spending another year in the same class; so, I never took that risk ever! I did not take a liking for her but went with the flow, given the underlying semantics of mandatory education at that age.

One fine morning, she tasked my hero with a seemingly straightforward question of proving the two drawn triangles congruent. The question did not bother me that much that day as I was a non-participative audience keen on watching the two warring parties in action.

He took the stage with aplomb and with what looked to me like some mystical drawings from the bygone Egyptian era, solved the question with a flourish of the white chalk that he then broke into two.

The teacher was suddenly aghast; pain and disbelief flooding her face. She looked around desperately at all of us as if something indescribable, uncomprehending had just occurred. I was stunned and perplexed because to my inept brain, this reaction was just opposite to the congratulatory handshake that I had imagined.

I looked around trying to make sense of this oddity. When I asked my neighbour, she just glanced at the blackboard, lighting a path for me to follow. The 'congruent' in the teacher's question was struck off and replaced with another word that I had no idea of then.

He had proven the triangles to be 'similar' than 'congruent', highlighting not only a huge departure from the teacher's ask but a potential inaccuracy in the question itself.

It is no surprise then that this youngster went on to become the CEO of a Fortune 500 company.

Child was the father of ~~man~~ teacher, in this case.

Misplaced horror

The eight classes in school daily, each lasting forty-five minutes, were delivered by a mix of teachers, unique in their teaching styles. Most of the teachers meant business and that translated into assignments, tests, and serious studies.

Learning Hindi was exacting, except for students from the northern parts of India. Given our almost negligible understanding of the language due to our southern base, most of us felt smothered by the relentless barrage of grammar that was lobbed at us to learn.

While this itself was making my life demanding, the Hindi schooling at home by my non-Hindi speaking parents, with local accents, ensured an unimaginable, gruelling confrontation with my teacher, almost every time.

Our Hindi teacher was a stout lady with a look that was positively dangerous; hence, avoidance was the key.

The peculiarity of her teaching was that she alternated her classes with schoolbook teaching and horror story telling. This meant that if she delivered a Hindi class today, the next day would be a horror genre story telling day. She had a quiver of creepy stories to regale us with, which resulted in squeamish nightmares for me, post every sunset, especially when walking below the banyan tree or hearing the howling wind.

The real twist was yet to come. With her quota of stories exhausted and her thirst still not quenched, she found an easy medium in us to amuse her with more horror stories. And she had a great plan. Every alternate class was reserved for this story telling. Each student was supposed to search, read, and prepare a story by any means possible.

When asked, students who had a great story to tell raised their hands to be noticed. She would then pick anyone at random with her finger pointing at the unlucky student and the forty-five-minute session would start. Other students would bide their time and luck, given the lottery system worked solely in her head. Harsh punishment beckoned if the story was not to her liking.

One of us from our 'famous trio' figured a way out to solve this raffle system wherein he would be spared this exercise of storytelling, or so he thought. Per his analysis and close observation spread over a period of two months, he had noticed that students who raised their hands were rarely asked to narrate their story.

On the D-day, when the time came to raise hands for the story narration for our teacher, my dear friend was a tad too fast for his own liking. He raised his hand confidently only to realize that he was singularly the only one to do so in the sweepstake party that day. The teacher looked at him, the dreaded finger rising in slow motion, imploring him to come to the front of the class to narrate his horror account.

Stuck at odd angles, sweat glistening from the forehead, the sheep stepped slowly forward towards the slaughterhouse—his calculation had backfired magnificently. He had no story to tell or share. Shivering profusely, he maintained a dignified silence till the sound of a resounding slap reverberated through the whole classroom.

The class was stunned into silence. Our dear friend, holding his reddened cheek, walked back silently to his seat, avoiding all the gazes and glares directed at him.

The news of this horror genre activity reached the principal's office, and the resulting outcome ensured that those alternate classes were replaced by Hindi studies.

My friend had played an individual gamble that he lost but unknowingly had won the collective war for the entire class.

Samosa on the boundary

My school was located at the end of our colony. It was a four-storied complex with a huge playground at the back. All this was enclosed by a six-feet compound wall running from one end to the other.

North of this wall lay a small canal filled with muddy water. It was not a great sight to behold, but most of us loved it for a simple reason—the samosa shack that shared this common boundary with the school. The small mainland on the opposite side was connected to this shop by a cement block thrown haphazardly across.

The proprietor worked in tandem with his wife to make these tasty treats, starting at about ten in the morning till six in the evening. The potatoes used for the filling could be seen lazing around, to be boiled per requirement. Their shape and size did not matter—the taste did.

There was no one in the colony who had not tasted these samosas; they were very delicious, retained the same taste since eons, were economical in pricing, and most importantly, the shack was the go-to place to reduce hunger pangs.

While we used to get our lunch from home, we still had the hots for these savoury snacks, the smell of which wafted over the compound wall to our waiting nostrils, precisely as if on cue, when we opened our lunch boxes.

The problem was that the school had banished these luring samosas from its realm. The consumption of these tasty snacks was an affront to the school's guidelines. Anybody seen breaking this rule incurred the wrath of the principal, including but not relegated to detention outside the principal's office for a week.

Our team of friends was never a stickler for rules. With that thought in mind, a supportive pat on the back, a furtive glance towards the staff room for observation, my friend would face the wall clasping his hands behind his back. This was my cue to place my foot on the miniscule hand deck thus created, jump onto the parapet of the compound wall, hoist myself up, and convey our collective requirements to the 'samosa wallah'.

Holding my breath for all the right reasons, I would throw the collected samosa packet and jump down to enjoy the labour of my hard work. This was a regular weekly feature that we rarely denied ourselves.

Luck has this bad habit of running out at the most crucial junctures. One day, while I was in the midst of jumping, post-delivery of the package, a loud warning shout signaled movement in the principal's office towards our smuggling den. All that I heard after was the frantic movement of rustling and then running feet towards the classrooms, leaving me stranded atop the compound wall.

Having no other option, since spending time outside the principal's office was a big no-no, I scaled the wall to land on the shack's floor. Unfortunately, the lady of the shack had replaced the man at that very moment when I descended. Touching down was a great mess since I fell on her lap, sending both of us tumbling together on the bare floor.

Hearing the commotion and thud, the samosa wallah came running and seeing the baffling sight frantically searched for the stick he used to keep stray dogs at bay. Fortunately, when he saw me get up, recognition flooded, and the stick was kept at abeyance.

With no money in my pocket, samosas lost to my traitor friends, and my school bag in the classroom, I had no option but to wait out the whole afternoon. Sympathising with my distressed state, the samosa wallah was kind enough to supply me with his quota of samosas for lunch.

The next day saw me outside the principal's office, a pilgrimage that lasted seven days. I looked the perfect epitome of the patriotic Indian during the British Raj—betrayed, wounded, and captured.

Cat and mice

Dad was not a strict father, but like most of the senior male folks that time, gave the appearance of a very stern person, not to be easily trifled with. That show of appearance was successful since we were fearful of him. Maintaining our distance from him became the order of the day.

We came from a family of food connoisseurs. All of us loved food but we brothers had taken this liking to the next level with our appreciation for non-vegetarian delights. The problem was that my dad was a pure vegetarian who abhorred even the slightest mention of anything related to animal food. With dad around, it was hence impossible to enjoy these worldly treats.

Imagine our ecstasy then when we were informed that dad had gotten a new role which entailed travelling to faraway horizons —trips lasting a couple of days or more. The cat now just needed to be away when the mice played. We couldn't hide the grins on our faces which surprised dad no ends.

Mom remained a minor deterrent but nothing that we couldn't overcome. We brought her to our side by showing her the promised life—life with her friends late into the afternoons, no lunch worries for dad, easy evenings, and late-night movie binges on TV with us. Mom, though also a vegetarian, flipped three sixty degrees, and our team was complete. Her children were her world; so, if it was non-veg that kept them happy, so be it—she would buy, prepare, and cook.

Dad's travels were ad hoc, he had no prior intimation of where and when. To solve this fear of the unknown, he prepared a travel suitcase to be kept in the office. This was the icing on the cake for his traitorous team at home. The moment he called to convey his travel plans to us, the otherwise quiet house transformed into a boisterous musical party hall and an aromatic restaurant-like kitchen unit rolled into one.

News confirmed, one of us would trudge to the marketplace to buy meat, the other would go to the vegetable vendor to get the necessary ingredients, and mom would prepare the kitchen for the onslaught. It was a great time for the three of us. Between greedy food intakes we watched movies and sports matches late into the night without a worry in the world.

Those were blissful days and nights, until that fateful day when the inevitable happened. We were enjoying our meal as usual—the smell of fish permeating the air and music blaring loudly from the gramophone recorder when we heard a loud perceptible knock on the door. I opened the door to a view that knocked me near senseless. In front of me was a man who had the exact likeness to my dad.

There was no escape from the commotion that followed. We were berated, scolded, hints of conspiracies unfolded, leaving us with pangs of guilt for this treachery.

Dad forgot all this the next day; we did not.

Non-vegetarian food never entered our premises post this altercation; we went to it instead, in the restaurants that dotted the town.

Trainacation

Vacation time was awaited with bated breath, all through my school years. It started in April and lasted till June, a period of two months. It was the most exciting time of my childhood because it was the official seal not to be amongst the books.

The week before the vacations used to be the toughest to manage. Days would appear to extend into months. Everything seemed to have taken a slow-motion hue, except for the vacation assignments peppered across the class blackboard by the teachers responsible for their subjects.

Add to that, jotting questions down in my homework notebook was nothing short of torture. They were many and my fingers craved for forgiveness and mercy by the time I had finished writing a few of them. I just passed on the merciless baton from the teacher to my fingers and they shamefully went back to do my bidding. Sometimes I could feel them shivering due to this rebuff.

When the final day arrived, we would gather at the school gate, with promises and goodbyes shared in equal numbers—promises of plans for the break with friends closer home and goodbyes to all those too physically distant to meet during the holidays. Tears would copiously overflow for the latter because we wouldn't be seeing each other for quite some time.

With these heartfelt dramatics out of the way, I spent time galivanting through the neighbourhood on borrowed bicycles, playing sports, walking leisurely across the colony streets, and generally making merry with my friends.

While this time was great fun predominantly, there was a customary heartburn as well. One of the biggest spoilsports was this vacation opportunity that Dad would use to plan his annual trip back home. This meant losing at least a month of vacation time traveling to our native state Kerala, meeting relatives after a year or more, and generally not having friends for the fun and frolic that was the mainstay of this break.

Not that I had a say in this. Decisions were merely passed on to the younger folks for execution. With a tepid heart, I would pack my bags and fearfully wait for the day to board the long journey back to my roots. The voyage took about two and a half days from start to finish, sitting and sleeping in the air-conditioned coupe that could house four members—a boon for us since we were a family of four. No outsiders were hence allowed inside. This was our own private space for the next couple of days.

While the first couple of hours were spent checking the coupe and the various lighting systems inside it, the next few were spent lazing around before boredom took over. This resulted in walks across the length of the compartment, casting furtive glances across the other coupes and inhabitants housed in them.

We did not have the benefit of calling the local pantry for food, snacks, or any juices. We had our own homecooked food for consumption. This was supposed to be a brilliant idea by one of the elders in the family since food wouldn't spoil in an air-conditioned environment. Sadly, for us kids, dreams of having novel, outside food were flung on the walls of hope and shattered into the grounds of despair.

Window seat was the privileged seat to be in. There were two window seats that both of us brothers would make a point of hijacking without a second thought. The problem was when the train took a steep turn on the track and one of us fought with the other to chance on the view of the beautiful curve that the train took.

After some trips, smartness took over and the combat was for the window seat that had the greater probability of a better view. My brother won most of the times since he had adequate support from other family members. I rarely stood a chance. The only silver lining was the seat sharing when the opportune moment arrived to enjoy the view together. I would literally be kissing the window, holding my brother by the scruff of his collar for the panoramic spectacle.

Finally, after a non-eventful journey of a couple of days and more, we would reach our village early in the morning. After the customary greetings, we would venture out to investigate the neighbourhood.

Gently, as the days progressed, the simplicity of village life, the clean air, and the treelined fields with acres of unrestricted view got the better of me. I fell in love with my heritage all over again, just like on previous trips.

The angst at my father for separating me from my friends back home changed to unadulterated respect. He, despite coming from this rural setup, had established himself successfully in a big city and taken proactive, selfless responsibility of his family, shaping their futures, one month at a time.

Family was always home, home was always family—both thick as thieves—an inseparable combination. I am glad that I was privy to this forgotten altruistic world that now is just a word.

Pitter patter

Rainy days gave me a natural high. I couldn't wait to watch the lightning glistening across the stadium, hear the enormous clap of thunder, and follow the splinters of the splattering rain falling all around me. The monsoon months were rejuvenating to the senses, the cold air a respite from the heat wave that rattled us throughout the day.

What I loved most about the monsoon was school time. Shivering in my shorts, clutching my multi-coloured umbrella, I would run across the street towards school, trying to beat the rain whipping down on me relentlessly. I would naturally lose, but the run would revitalize me for the day ahead. It was fun to jump across the puddles of water, avoid smearing my uniform, and reach school a little drenched, but high on hope and happiness at nature's awesome magic.

The school corridors would be wet with the rain pounding the open balconies on all the floors, the staircase would be moist with the touch of the sodden hands of other students, and the class floor would be sparkly with the footprints of the moist shoes.

'Frictionless' took an altogether new meaning. I was a professional skater when I ran, slipped, and slid on the wet corridor floor to the mortification of the lesser mortals who were afraid to partake of this fun. The shoe soles did take a beating, but it was a small price to pay for this amusement.

The wet staircase balustrade was another indoor gaming option that I used to my heart's content. I would lean on the handrail, pull my knees up to avoid hitting the steps on my way down, and just glide down the guardrail to the landings one by one till I reached the ground level.

While I looked forward to some missed classes due to the teacher's absence, missing out on the sports class was a big damper to an otherwise beautiful time. The school playground would be wet and soggy thus disallowing any of us to play our usual games of football, hockey, or cricket. The cemented basketball court suffered the same fate. To me they appeared melancholic due to underuse.

Lunch time filled the classroom with the discordance of different voices talking, shouting, and opening tiffin boxes simultaneously. The lunch was generously shared across, and by the time it was over, the classroom did not smell its usual self. Instead, it smelled like a buffet, the smelly concoction ranging from okay to bad.

For most of us, rainy days meant enjoying in nature's lap. It meant spending time outside, trying to imprison the tiny droplets in our palms, putting handmade paper boats to sail in the small water islands formed on undulated streets, and savouring this moment with the environment. There was never the fear of falling sick since mom would be ready with a towel and a hot cup of turmeric milk in hand to offset anything that may destroy this simple joy.

The rains are still the same, but they seem to fall with a lot of fury and anger now. Maybe, they are just missing their fearless tiny tot partners; the innocent ones who always welcomed them down.

First division

Nine years of school passed in a blur. The dreaded tenth class arrived and with it, the fear of the much-publicized, alarming board exams loomed big. For me, whose student life was spent wrestling the study demons, this seemed to indicate the end of a non-illustrious student life.

My father never had the fortune of seeing his younger child obtain sixty percentile or more in any of the nine years that I was in school. While I did not see red ever thankfully, the marks hovered around the late fifties but never reached the much treasured first division that marked the arrival of the intelligent student.

It was not as if I had not persisted hard to reach the coveted grade. It just never worked out in my favour. Sadly, I couldn't even blame my genes for fear of serious family repercussions.

My dad had given up hope and resigned himself to the reality that his son would land a mere fifty in his board exams. This hermit-like acceptance kept him grounded and comforted me no ends.

Board exams arrived a little too soon for my liking. Mostly the questions across all subjects seemed alien, leading me to believe that the examiner would suffer the same feeling when reading my answers.

A majority of my answers and solutions, especially those in the science stream subjects, were very different from what my other classmates had arrived at. In fact, I was the only one holding the banner of exclusivity amongst all my peers.

Exam results were out in the month of April. We, the 'famous trio', trudged together towards the noticeboard where the results were displayed for all to see. Knowing my many warring antagonists, I was sure that they were busy seeing my marks first before they went on to theirs.

The walk to the noticeboard outside the principal's office was the slowest trudge that I ever had made till then. It was as if a heavy weight was pressed on my back and the burden of it all was slowing me down drastically. When I looked around, I saw that my other friends seemed to have heavier weights because they were following me, lagging by a yard or so.

The notice board loomed ahead, and the crowd made way just as the sea parted when Moses raised his staff. The three of us offered silent prayers to our respective lords and let our deeds decide our marks. Two seconds later, I saw my friends beaming with unbridled joy. Feeling a little envious, I looked at them and they voiced together that we had made it through. Hearing that was a huge relief, but the next sentence elevated my spirit a notch further—the three of us had passed in first division! That too, in the top seventies.

My gait changed, my chest puffed out as I walked back home to my nervous mother waiting to hear the imminent disastrous news. Our neighbour, who had a high eighty score to show off, also made a beeline to our barbed wire boundary wall to enjoy the commotion that would wreck in our otherwise normally quiet household. Everybody's confidence in my ability to not surprise was nerve-racking. It made me feel sheepish and unsettled, draining the colour off from my face.

My mom saw this change first and went ballistic with her sobs. She had assumed that I had failed to make the cut. Before I could say anything, she ran into the house and dialed dad's landline number. She conveyed the news in a hardline tone ensuring that dad understood what the next course of action needed to be when he arrived home hastily from the office.

With the phone receiver thumped down in the cradle, she brushed past me, but I caught her by the hand and relayed the happy news to her.

Her facial muscles twitched, the stiff upper lip curved to show the beginning of shock and surprise together and then automatically course corrected to an impish smile.

She hugged me tight and holding my hand walked outside with the same smile plastered on her face. Getting a hint of the anticlimax, our neighbour made an unobtrusive, swift retreat.

Dad arrived thirty minutes later with the same expressionless, nonchalant face that gave nothing away. He listened to mom's happy tidings, looked at me standing behind her, came forward, and shook my hands.

I felt the warmth of that handshake that highlighted his congratulatory gesture. This was followed by his one-liner—"Congratulations! You got a first division."

Old habits die hard. Next year, my grades withered, and the late fifties took over again.

My parents couldn't complain. I had achieved the impossible. By pure providence, I had got the timing right. You are a hero if you deliver when it matters the most, just like me then.

Two schools

The two schools in our colony were as disparate as chalk and cheese. One was a convent run by Roman catholic nuns while the other, by the government. While they were hardly five hundred metres apart, these schools stood opposite, as if to mock each other's presence in this world.

We, the convent studs, blatantly, but jokingly, looked down upon the government school—a school with eleven a.m. to three p.m. timings—one that seemed to copy our dress code, yet had an economical fee structure, and looked to be more forgiving of its naughty students.

In the rare event that our paths crossed, we would either ignore, pick a fight, or heckle the government school's students for the fun of it. This continued for many years, and we unwittingly made some unforgiving enemies.

The real catastrophe struck when we passed our tenth grade. Our school, for all its goodness, did not offer higher secondary education. The only two options available were either to apply to schools outside our colony or to the school opposite ours.

Our methodical pulverisation had bitten the dirty and unforgiving dust. In all our overconfident smartness, we had been ignorant that the government-run school provided higher secondary education.

With my tenth-grade marks, there were no schools sane enough to take me under their tutelage; they all had a reputation to protect furiously, especially from such seedy non-starters.

The one school that eventually took us in was relatively new, and twenty kilometres away in the city. We went with the tide, organised transport, and left our homes at five-thirty in the morning for the eight-a.m. classes.

From a life of comfort, where we woke up to the second bell warning and then sauntered to school, to this life was not exactly a demotion; it was downright humiliation for all of us.

Our ego was bruised, and we had nowhere else to go, so we appealed to our parents collectively to see if we could be admitted into the school opposite our convent one.

The tables had turned and how. We were now at the mercy of the very school that we had spent a lifetime sportingly mocking. Much to our pleasant surprise it did not turn a blind eye to our request. Instead, to our utter shock, it created an entirely new section just to accommodate our batch.

We were given a rousing welcome on the first day at the campus by everyone. It was a celebration of sorts, and the initiation was so natural that we never felt like outsiders even for a moment.

Our mockery was bested by something much bigger and better—humanity's humane heart—a rarity now!

Time travel

Graduation day arrived. It was a day of meeting friends, classmates, teachers, and everybody else who had played an important part in our evolution from childhood to adolescence.

It was also a time to say goodbyes because we would be going the separate ways that life had preordained for us. This involved a bit of despair since the solid cocoon of school time was being replaced by the boundless ocean of life, with no safety net below us.

Post the customary greetings and addresses by the principal and other stakeholders, we were left free to meet with our peers. Most of them shared their vivid dreams—dreams that foretold great, bright, successful futures, and a life that boasted of all the best that it could offer.

I had no inkling of what the outside world had in store for me. Love for sports and a happy-go-lucky attitude was all that I possessed. Hearing my classmates talk about their well laid out plans was dampening my spirits and making me miserable in that company.

Reaching home, I encountered my father first up at the door. Looking at my downtrodden face and my predicament thereafter, he went and brought his much-worn singular Seiko watch. Clasping it on my wrist he said, "Make time your best friend by not rushing it, but waiting for it. Everything will fall in place eventually, it has to. Let this watch always remind you of this unquestionable truth."

Years later, just like other improbably difficult stand-offs, while navigating the city's potholed roads, braving the snarling and honking traffic, this advice from dad has been a life saviour. The cool-headedness, patience, and the ability to steer calmly under these excruciating conditions is the most intangible and ultimate gift from my dad.

Looking back, post some hiccups, the three of us ultimately did well in life. We have been fairly successful in our chosen or forced vocations, creating a happy, satisfactory environment for our family and well-wishers.

The busyness, lifestyle changes, procrastinations, and memory lapses cost us thirty years of lost correspondence. Until one day, thanks to my daughter, in a long-lost shore outside India, two of us met to relive our past.

It was just like the old times—the heartfelt hugs, the smiles, the laughter, the memories—nothing had changed. One thing led to the other. Finally, the missing piece in our beautifully intricate friendship fell into place, when I bumped into the third from our group on social media.

The 'famous trio' was reborn in an alien realm where friendships, love, and relationships were easy to live and lose. Our old-world values brought us this far and soar further, unimpacted by this new-world charm.